WOODLAND
SCENE

Problems at Brock Manor

M.D.COCKETT

AuthorHouse™ UK
1663 Liberty Drive
Bloomington, IN 47403 USA
www.authorhouse.co.uk
UK TFN: 0800 0148641 (Toll Free inside the UK)
UK Local: 02036 956322 (+44 20 3695 6322 from outside the UK)

Because of the dynamic nature of the Internet, any web addresses or links contained in this book may have changed
since publication and may no longer be valid. The views expressed in this work are solely those of the author and do
not necessarily reflect the views of the publisher, and the publisher hereby disclaims any responsibility for them.

This book is printed on acid-free paper.

ISBN: 978-1-6655-9784-5 (sc)
ISBN: 978-1-6655-9785-2 (e)

Print information available on the last page.

Published by AuthorHouse 04/05/2022

The stories in this book are based on the "Woodland Scene" range of Soft-toys designed by Lin Cockett. The whole range of
18" tall Soft-toys can be bought as "Tip-Top" Toy patterns from Cockett Crafts which include detailed making instructions.
Other books containing short stories of each of the other "Woodland Scene" animals are available.
Soft-Toy catalogues can be obtained by writing to:-

COCKETT CRAFTS. 1 Ryelands Grove, Leominster.
Herefordshire HR6 8QA
Tel: (01568)-613697
ISBN 1 874294 02 X Paperback edition
revised edition 2009

Published by:
Tip-Top Publications. 1 Ryelands Grove, Leominster
Herefordshire HR6 8QA (Tel: 01568-613697)
© 1991 M.D.Cockett

authorHOUSE®

ACKNOWLEDGEMENTS

With thanks to my late wife, Linda (Lin) who designed the wonderful range of collectable soft-toys from which my inspiration was generated to write these stories, and who drew some of the illustrations.

ILLUSTRATIONS

WOODLAND SCENE

Problems at Brock Manor

by

M.D. COCKETT

CONTENTS

She read the note pinned to the door

CHAPTER 1

BLANCHE BADGER APPEARS

Bessie Beaver came to work in a very good mood. One might even say it was an exceptionally good mood. She had been presented with a 'Service of Excellency' Medal, for her work at the Manor, only the Friday before.

There had been a special party in her honor, and everyone from the village and staff of Brock Manor had been there.

This morning she breezed round the Manor doing all her chores, making sure all her staff knew what they were to do that day.

As she passed by Silvia Shrew, she teasingly said, "That's an unusually strong perfume you're wearing today, isn't it?"

Silvia said that she never wore strong perfumes to work, and the funny thing was, she thought one of the other members of the staff was wearing it.

It was a very strong perfume, and it wafted about, all over the Manor. It could be detected for days, even on the Thursday which was the half-day for the staff, when they all left, as usual, at lunch-time. Bastien was left in the Manor with Bessie Beaver, and for about an hour they discussed the work required for the next week. As Bessie left for home, Bastien remarked that her new perfume was very strong.

"It's not mine," said Bessie, "I've not been able to find out who *is* wearing it. I'm sure it's not one of the staff."

The following morning, Bessie arrived for work as she had always done for the past thirty years, to find all the staff gathered in little groups, outside the front door of the Manor.

"What is going on?" enquired Bessie. "Why aren't you inside working? That's where you all should be."

"You'd better see this," said Silvia Shrew, pointing to a note pinned to the door.

The note read:

'No staff required until

further notice

The Manor is now closed'

It was not signed.

Bessie scratched her head. That was most unusual. In her thirty years of working at the Manor, she had never known anything like this to happen before and Bastien had not mentioned it when they talked yesterday.

"But where *is* Bastien? I was with him yesterday afternoon, but he never mentioned anything to me," said a bewildered Bessie out loud.

"Has anybody checked round the Manor, the other entrances, windows and such like?"

Bobby Bunny had done all that. He had even checked the new pane of glass which had replaced the one found broken after Bessie's party.*

"Has anybody seen Bastien?" enquired Bessie again.

Every head shook slowly. Nobody had seen him.

"I suppose you had all better go home until we can sort this out," said Bessie. "It really is quite strange. Now off you all go."

"Not you Bobby," said Bessie, as the other servants sauntered off, grumbling among themselves. "We'd better have a fresh look around together."

They checked every window and door, even the secret entrance to the Manor.

Book 1: "The Badgers of Brock Manor: Chapter 6

All were secure and nowhere could they find any trace of Bastien.

"Let's have another look at that note," suggested Bobby, "The writing doesn't look like Bastien's, his writing *does* slope to the left, but it is much larger. It looks to me as if a female hand has written it and it has that same perfume smell on it as well."

"Well. it wasn't any of my staff," said Bessie, "and *I* certainly didn't write it."

They failed to see a curtain move just above and to the right of them. If they had, they might have caught a glimpse of a black and white face and a blue dress.

"I'm going to check all the sheds before I go," said Bobby, "Are you coming with me? I can't see what else we can do."

"I may as well," said Bessie, "It is all rather confusing to me. There must be a simple explanation."

They checked every shed on the estate, and at the very last one, as they opened the door, a scruffy figure rolled out.

It took them both by surprise. It was Bastien Badger!

"What on earth are you doing in there?" Bessie asked, kneeling down to help him up.

"I've been locked out." said a distraught Bastien, "Aunt Blanche has taken over the Manor. When you all went yesterday, I was in the garden, and heard the door slam. I thought it was the wind."

"That didn't bother me, as the doors are not self-locking, but when I went to open it, I found it was stuck. In fact it had been locked from the inside."

He continued: "Every door into the Manor had been secured, and as I was trying to figure out how to get in, Aunt Blanche opened an upstairs window and shouted down to me. She told me to clear off, as the Manor should *not* belong to me, because it should have been left to Basil, my elder brother, in spite of what my father's Will stated. I had nowhere to go, so I slept in this shed."

"You'd better come and stay with me," said Bessie.

"You're most welcome to stay with us as well," said Bobby, immediately after Bessie.

"Thank you, but I'll not rest until I have regained possession of my inheritance," said Bastien, "but how am I going to do that?"

They persuaded Bastien to go home with Bessie and she made him have a bath, while she washed all his grubby clothes.

Bobby came round during the afternoon with some of his old gardening clothes, so that Bastien, at least, had something to wear, as he had no other clothes with him, and he couldn't get hold of any, because they were all in the Manor.

They all had a drink, and discussed how to regain possession of the Manor. It was impossible to storm the Manor and try to take it by force, so they had to think of something else.

"We could prevent anyone going to the Manor, so that they would run out of provisions. Aunt Blanche could not survive long without fresh food," suggested Bastien.

I don't think that's a good idea," said Bobby, "because there's a garden full of fresh vegetables and fruit. She could easily survive a siege until the Winter, for she could slip out late at night, and collect whatever she wanted.

"Of course you're right," said Bastien, "and we have our own water supply at the Manor too. I don't know what to do."

"Could we gain access to the Manor through the secret entrance?" asked Bessie. "You remember those Weasels did, didn't they?*

Both Bastien and Bobby remembered that incident well. "But Aunt Blanche knows of the entrance because she told the Weasels about it, so it wouldn't be a surprise, and I remember locking it well after the attack." said Bastien.

"I wonder," said Bobby. "Shall we take a look?"

Book 1: The Badgers of Brock Manor: Chapter 4

That evening, the two of them took one of Bessie's torches, and cautiously entered the grounds of the Manor, edging their way to the secret entrance, to prevent being seen.

They arrived at the wall with the secret entrance and found the door tightly closed.

It would not budge!

It only took Bobby a few more pushes.

CHAPTER 2

BASTIEN THE BRAVE

Bobby began to shake the door of the secret entrance, but was stopped by Bastien.

"Do it quietly, she'll hear us," he whispered.

Bobby carried on, saying that if Aunt Blanche did hear them, she would probably investigate the noise, and they could catch her. It took Bobby only a few more pushes, and the door burst open and swung inwards, slamming against the inner wall of the tunnel with a loud *'crash!'*

"That's done it," said Bastien, wide-eyed with anticipation, "She's *bound* to have heard *that!*"

They waited in complete silence for a few minutes, watching the entrance, but nobody came to investigate. They entered the tunnel and slowly crawled along it until they came to the crossroads.

"To the left is a dead-end," whispered Bastien, "Straight on, the tunnel comes out near my old office. In fact, it comes out in my new one. To the right is another dead end. It goes into a large chamber which we used for storing things. I can't remember what's in there now."

"Let's take a look then." advised Bobby. "There's no harm in looking is there?"

"Quite right." said Bastien, already moving in that direction.

With Bobby holding the torch, they went through the short tunnel, and entered the large chamber. The light from the torch lit up the whole area, and they both could see quite clearly. The chamber was cold, but not chilly or damp, and had a church-like quietness about it.

There wasn't much in the chamber, except some old sacking, some broken boxes and plenty of spider's webs, and a crate holding a few bottles of brandy, which must have been overlooked when the place was last cleared out.

"I think that I could stay here," said Bastien slowly. "Do you think that you could bring me some food and water in the mornings and evenings?"

"Yes, of course I can," answered Bobby. "Are you staying here tonight then, for if you are, I'll have to tell Bessie for she'll want her torch back?"

"Perhaps I'd better go back and tell her what I'll be doing." said Bastien.

Bessie thought it was a silly idea, him sleeping in a cold dark place like the chamber, when he could have a nice warm bed at her place, for as long as he liked.

"What about your washing, and good warm food?" she asked. "You can't stay in the chamber for a long time without fresh air, fresh food and plenty of batteries for the torch."

"Bobby could keep me supplied with what I wanted," was the curt reply.

Bessie was quite taken back with his short remark, but realized what he must be going through, being thrown out of his home with nothing, and by his own Aunt, as well.

He was obviously determined to recover his possessions quickly.

"Oh! I'm sorry," said Bastien, realizing he had almost been rude to Bessie, "I'd quite forgotten your kindness in putting me up and your willingness to help me."

"Don't you worry 'bout that," said a ruffled Bessie. "You must be under quite a strain. I'll do what I can to help."

"We must devise a plan to get back into the Manor. I'll stay here tonight, if that's all right with you," said Bastien apologetically, "but in the morning, I'll get some supplies together and think out what my plan of action should be."

In the morning, Bastien was slow to get up. He'd found it so comfortable in one of Bessie Beaver's soft beds, and had slept so well after one of her evening meals. "I must be mad," he thought to himself, "to want to stay in some cobwebby cold chamber, but I have to find some way of getting back into the Manor."

By lunchtime he had borrowed a torch, a spare bulb, some spare batteries, a sleeping bag, a large flask and some warm clothing.

Bessie had put some hot nourishing soup in the flask and made a large amount of sandwiches which would last some time. She wrapped them up, to keep them fresh.

When evening came, Bastien set off, arriving at the Manor, just as darkness was beginning to fall, so he would not easily be seen from the windows of the Manor.

He found the door to the secret tunnel, exactly as they had left it the night before. It opened easily and he was able to take all his equipment into the chamber without any problems.

He selected a corner in the chamber, free of spider's webs and laid out some of the broken boxes to make a temporary bed, so that he would not have to sleep directly on the floor.

On top of these, he laid the sleeping bag and hid his spare batteries, bulbs and food in another corner, out of sight of any possible intruders.

Then, laying fully dressed on his makeshift bed, with the torch switched off, he started to try and work out how he could get from the chamber into the Manor proper, without making too much noise.

Around midnight, he went back to the tunnel crossroads and turned right into the tunnel that went directly to his new office to check if the exit might be unlocked.

He tried the door, but it was locked solid.

He felt all round the edges of the door to try to find any hidden catches or anything unusual which might allow him to open the door.

There was nothing, so he returned to his chamber and decided he would get into his sleeping bag as it was getting quite cold. He could then have a long think about the problem in relative warmth and comfort. It would be easier to think without the distractions of Bessie or Bobby being around.

That is why he had turned down all the generous offers from them, when they asked him to stay with them, so he could think, without interruption.

As he lay in the total darkness, he began to focus his mind on his problem, and he studied his situation very carefully.

He had to get into the Manor, without making any noise, and without being detected. As far as he knew, the only occupant was his Aunt Blanche.

He liked his Aunt and wondered how he would overpower her, if and when, he was able to. It wasn't very gentlemanly attacking ladies, particularly your own relations, but then he thought, sometimes those that are the closest to you, are the ones that hurt you the most.

The next thing he knew was when he woke up. It was pitch black. He realized where he was, switched on his torch, and looked at his watch.

It said 5:23 in the morning. He had only been asleep for a few hours, but he felt quite refreshed and his mind was alert. It was chilly and deathly silent in the chamber. No sounds at all could be heard.

He decided to walk through the tunnel system from end to end to see if there were any loose stones, wires or tools, anything he might be able to use.

A few minutes after 6, he returned to eat his sandwiches, and drink his hot soup, kindly supplied by Bessie the night before.

He had just finished when he heard a dull scraping noise coming from somewhere in the tunnel.

The fur on the back of his neck stood up noticeably, and looking for an escape route, he realized he was trapped. He turned out his torch and waited with his heart pounding.

The scraping noise slowly became louder and louder as it came nearer and nearer, until Bastien knew that who or whatever was making the noise, was quite close to him.

A dull light flickered in the tunnel leading to his chamber, lighting up all the spiders webs and broken boxes and, as the light moved in the tunnel, so the shadows of the spiders webs and the broken boxes, danced on the walls of his chamber.

It was quite frightening.

Bastien held his breath. He could feel a trickle of cold sweat, running down his snout, making him want to sneeze. He managed not to for a short while, then couldn't hold the sneeze back any longer.

"Aieeetishooooo!" rebounded round his chamber, then echoed throughout the tunnel.

"Is that you, Bastien?" came a startled voice. "It's only me, Bobby Bunny. I've come to see if you're alright."

"Thank goodness it's only you," said Bastien, his heart still pounding. "I didn't expect you'd be coming this early."

They exchanged flasks and sandwiches, hot for cold and new for old.

"Have you found the way in yet?" asked Bobby.

"I've checked every brick in the tunnels, and the door to my office is locked solid. I really don't know where to look next."

Bobby looked round the chamber. It was not a place he wished to stay in on his own, and he admired Bastien's courage in sleeping there.

The boxes slipped and crashed to the floor.

CHAPTER 3

BOBBY'S DISCOVERY

As Bobby looked round the cold, creepy chamber, he noticed something hanging from the ceiling and pointed to it.

"What's that doing there?" he enquired, shining his torch at the ceiling.

They piled the old boxes and the crate in a heap, and Bastien climbed onto them gingerly and, by stretching, could just reach the hanging thing. It was an old electric cable. The bulb had long since disappeared, but the wire and holder were still in good condition and a piece of broken cord hung from it.

"What can we do with that?" asked Bobby, scratching his head.

"I don't knooooowooooowooow," said Bastien, as the pile of boxes wobbled.

They slipped and crashed to the floor, making Bobby jump out of the way, to avoid them, and a falling Bastien.

In doing so, Bobby dropped his torch, which rolled behind some old sacking hanging on one of the walls, thankfully staying alight. He called out to Bastien to see if he was hurt, and was surprised when he heard Bastien's reply come from the ceiling and not the floor.

"I'm O.K., he called, "but get me down!"

He had jumped and grabbed hold of the cord, hanging from the light fixing, as the boxes tumbled from under his feet, and was hanging on to it. The holder came away from the ceiling, getting longer and longer, as it lowered him gently to the floor.

"Well, that was lucky," said Bobby. "I was beginning to wonder how to get you down. It's a long piece of cord isn't it? Perhaps we can use it somehow."

The cord was quite rigid and certainly strong enough to take the weight of Bastien, but as soon as Bastien let go of it, to look for something to cut it with, it slowly, along with the cable, retracted towards the ceiling.

Meanwhile, in the kitchen, which was directly above the chamber, the electric wiring, under Bastien's weight, had pulled several lights off the walls. They had fallen into the metal sink and onto the floor and the bulbs had exploded one by one, waking Aunt Blanche from an uneasy sleep. Thinking she was being attacked, she hurried to the kitchen and switched on the lights to see what had caused the noise.

No lights came on though, for the instant she touched the switch, a broken light bulb shorted-out with a flash, and the fuse box, above her head, blew out with a sharp '*bang*'! making her utter a stifled "*ooh!*"

Aunt Blanche was frightened. She was in a house which she had seized by cunning and it was dark, the lights had all fused and she thought someone was shooting at her.

She inched along the wall as it was dark, paw over paw, as well as she could, glancing round the kitchen. There must be somebody there, for she could hear faint voices.

She searched the kitchen, but found no one, but she could still hear voices. Perhaps the place was haunted! Oh dear! What if it was the ghost of her brother, Sir Regnault?

That was silly. She didn't believe in ghosts. She went back to the stairs.

Bastien and Bobby were wondering what they might have done with the length of cord and strong cable, quite oblivious to the problems in the kitchen above them, and equally not knowing that their conversation was filtering into the kitchen, through the hole in the ceiling where the wire came through.

Bastien, not realizing the cord and cable had retracted into the ceiling, felt around for them in the dimmed light and could not find them.

"That's funny," he said, "They were here a few minutes ago."

"What were?" asked Bobby, walking over to retrieve the torch from behind the sacking.

"The cord and wire." said Bastien. "They have gone. Bring the torch, and shine it over here, and let's have a look for them."

As Bobby lifted the sacking up, to pick-up the torch, he discovered an opening in the wall, revealing a dark hole and the torch had rolled into the opening.

"Come here, quickly," he called to Bastien, "Look at this."

"I can't at the moment," said Bastien, "I need the torch to find the cord and cable."

"I think it may be your way into the Manor," said Bobby, shining the now retrieved torch into the opening, revealing a flight of curving stone steps, disappearing upwards.

"What!" exclaimed Bastien, "A way into the Manor from here. The only way I know is through the tunnels."

"Well, come and see for yourself," said Bobby excitedly, shining the light into the hole.

Bastien had one last feel around in the semi-dark for the cord and cable, shrugged his shoulders, then picked his way carefully, in the subdued light and avoiding the fallen boxes, to where Bobby had been standing by the sacking covering the hole in the wall.

"Where are you, then?" asked Bastien. "I can't see. It's suddenly gone dark. Too dark to see properly. Where have you gone?"

Bobby had taken the torch and was climbing the well-worn stone steps, leaving Bastien in total darkness. After a few seconds, he returned, full of excitement.

"There are two doors at the top." he puffed. "They are only small ones, but I think we could get through them."

"What are you talking about?" snapped Bastien. "Doors, what doors?"

"Take the torch and walk up those stone steps." advised Bobby, pointing to the opening in the wall, "Mind your head. It's low. Have a look for yourself."

Bastien did, returning seconds later. "You're right. I wonder where it comes out?"

"There's only one way to answer that question." said Bobby, "We'll have to open the doors and see."

Bastien went first and reached the first door. He shook it but it was solid. The other door was a few steps further up, but *that* door was loose and it rattled as he shook it.

Aunt Blanche was still in the kitchen above the room at that moment and heard the rattling of the door.

It was coming from Sir Regnault's old bedroom and she ran to the stairs. Was she beginning to believe in ghosts?

What with the strange voices in the kitchen, the mysterious knocking over and fusing of all the lights and now the rattling noise coming from his room, she was becoming a little worried.

"I've found the latch," said Bastien, which he clicked upwards and the door opened, noisily, inwards.

"I wonder where we are," he said to Bobby, and peered out from behind a row of clothes."

"The clothes look like your fathers' old clothes," said Bobby.

And they were, for the steps had led from his old wine cellar into Sir Regnault's dressing room, which adjoined the master bedroom.

"My father's clothes will fit me," said Bastien excitedly. "I'll put some on. Thank you for lending me your old working clothes, but these will be a better fit as yours are a little tight and not very comfortable.

He selected some of his father's clothes and, with Bobby holding the torch, changed in front of the full-length mirror.

Bobby gasped as the clothes made Bastien look just like his father.

"That's better," said Bastien, doing up the last button. "Now let's find out who's behind all this."

Aunt Blanche by this time, had summoned on her immense reserves of courage and ventured into the bedroom to investigate the noise.

As she entered the room, she saw a flickering shadowy figure of, she thought, Sir Regnault, coming through the large window.

It was actually a reflection of Bastien in his father's clothes, projected onto the window by the torch shining on the mirror.

She let out a shriek of total disbelief, and fell to her knees.

Bastien, hearing the shriek, turned away from the mirror and rushed into the bed-room, snatching the torch from Bobby Bunny's paw as he did so.

He saw a form laying on the floor and grabbed hold of it.

"Go away Reggie." a voice said, "Don't haunt me. You know the manor should belong to Basil and not Bastien."

Bobby had now entered the bedroom and saw Bastien holding his Aunt firmly by the arms. Bastien looked all bewildered and embarrassed and said: "Aunt Blanche, I'm sorry I was rough with you, but you have locked me out of the Manor and ..... oh!. I hope I haven't hurt you."

He paused to regain his breath and composure, and the strong smell of the perfume that Aunt Blanche was wearing, jogged his sub-conscious mind.

Things began to make sense. He recalled the broken window on the day of Bessie Beaver's party, and the strong scent in the Manor and on the notice .... Yes! It was the same scent.... So that's how she got in!*

*Book 1: The Badgers of Brock Manor: Chapter 6

He said in a slow deliberate voice. "It was you that broke the window in the back door, wasn't it? And then locked us out of the Manor. How did you manage that? Why did you do it?

His Aunt said nothing, but raised her snout defiantly, and her top lip began to quiver, revealing her strong teeth, and she began to growl quietly.

Bastien realized what was happening, and asked he again. "Why are you here? Couldn't you have let me know you were coming?"

His Aunt opened her lips slightly and growled through tightly clenched teeth, "Take your hands off me. Don't you ever try to frighten me like that again. I thought you were your father and he was haunting me. I saw his image in the window."

Bastien loosened his grip, and apologized, should he have hurt her, but he found it hard to believe that it was her, his Aunt, who had locked him out of his own home.

"It's about the ownership of the Manor isn't it," he asked in a saddened voice, quite sorry that he had inherited the house.

Blanche did not say a word, for her eyes were darting all around the room, looking for a way to escape, and Bastien could tell by her reaction, that he had got to the truth.

"If I let you go, promise me you won't run off," he said.

Again she raised her snout in a defiant gesture and Bastien knew she would make no such promise.

"Well, in that case, I'll have to make sure you can't escape. Help me to tie her legs," he called to Bobby. "She's about to ...."

He never finished the sentence for his Aunt had wriggled free, and was heading for the nearest door.

She reached it before Bastien had realized what was happening, opened it, and disappeared, slamming the door behind her with a loud *'Bang!'*

"We'll have to tie her up I'm afraid," said Bastien quietly to Bobby, as he turned the key in the lock of the door that Blanche has disappeared through. "Find something, and hurry up about it. She's gone into a cupboard and will soon realize it."

Bobby went back into the dressing room and took several strong ties from Sir Regnault's wardrobe. He returned just as Aunt Blanche began to hammer on the cupboard door.

"Let me out this minute," she demanded.

"I'm opening the door now," said Bastien, turning the key in the lock, but holding onto the door handle very firmly.

It was pitch black in the cupboard and he would not be able to see in clearly. Suddenly the door was wrenched from his strong grip as his Aunt burst out, through the doorway.

Bastien was prepared for her sudden action, and grabbed her round the waist, her momentum dragging them both to the floor.

"Quick, Bobby. Tie her legs while I hold her."

Bobby finally managed to hold Blanche's kicking legs still, long enough to slip a noose round them and to pull the tie tight.

"Now her arms." commanded Bastien.

Aunt Blanche struggled, for she was quite a strong Badger, equally as strong as Bastien and Bobby could not have restrained her without Bastien's help.

Even Bastien nearly let her go once. She was his Aunt and he did not feel right trapping her, but she had locked him out of his own home, causing him the discomfort of sleeping rough, and she had already broken free from his hold, just a few moments ago, and he was not going to let her escape again.

Finally, they tied her arms, with much struggling, cursing and attempted biting from Aunt Blanche, and they sat her down in a chair next to the window.

"Now we have you," said Bastien. "Aunt Blanche, you've got some explaining to do."

... and the form of Basil stood up.

CHAPTER 4

BASIL ARRIVES

Bastien and Bobby loosened the ties around Aunt Blanche's legs and led her, one on each arm, into the sitting room where they sat her down in a comfortable lounge chair.

They then tied her legs together again to make sure she didn't escape.

She was asked if she wanted anything to eat or drink, before Bastien started to question her about why she had not been happy about Sir Regnault's Will.

She replied, in a sharp voice, "I'm not discussing that now. I just want to go back to bed as it's too early in the morning and I don't usually get up at this time. Some strange banging noises in the kitchen woke me up."

Bastien snapped back. "It's getting lighter, as dawn is breaking. You've broken into my home, completely disrupted the running of the household, by locking everyone out, and preventing them from doing their work, and I want an explanation."

That was two days ago, which, for Bastien, had been quite dramatic. He had been locked out of his *own* home, was forced to spend an evening with one of his staff, and then had to spend another night in a dark chamber, alone.

It really was too much. He was determined to get to the bottom of why his Aunt was determined to possess the Manor, even if it took him all day to find out.

Bobby remarked that perhaps he should go and tell Bessie Beaver that Bastien had regained control of the Manor, and perhaps she could come back to work.

The house was in a mess, because Aunt Blanche had not bothered to do any house-work, so Bobby went to fetch Bessie Beaver.

Bobby returned shortly with her, and she grumbled about the mess the house was in, then Bastien called her into the lounge.

When she saw Aunt Blanche, all tied up, she curtsied and wished a "Good-morning Ma'am!"

Blanche took one look at Bessie and looked away.

It was bad enough being tied up, but to let the servants see her like this as well, was too much for this stubborn Badger.

Bessie Beaver was equally as embarrassed as Aunt Blanche.

"Don't worry about my Aunt Blanche," said Bastien, reassuringly to Bessie. "I want to talk to you about the return of the staff, so that we can get the Manor back to some sort of normality."

"Could you please contact the staff and ask them to come back to work. I'd send Bobby but Aunt Blanche might try to escape, and I need an extra pair of strong arms to help me restrain her."

At that moment, Bobby Bunny touched Bastien's arm and whispered something in his ear.

"I never thought of that," said Bastien. "Thank you Bobby!"

He then resumed his conversation with Bessie saying: "Perhaps we had better leave the staff for the time being," remembering what Bobby had just whispered to him. "Could you get the meals? I'm not *too* worried about keeping the place tidy, as I need to sort out this problem with my Aunt, and the fewer staff there are about, the better. If you would kindly do this for us, I would be very grateful."

Bessie didn't hesitate. "Of course, Bastien, anything you say."

When the evening came and Bessie was about to leave for home, Bastien said: "Bessie, Bobby was worried in case my brother, Basil, should turn up, so I think it is better if the staff were not asked back, for a while anyway. He must know by now that Aunt Blanche has taken over the Manor. I expect those Weasels have already told him, so he could be on his way here very soon."

"If he comes back to find everything looking normal, he'll think she's failed and he'll keep away. Bobby's not even going to mow the lawn to make it look as if we're not here. Perhaps you could vary the times when you come and go, so that he won't see you."

Aunt Blanche still wouldn't say a word. She just sat in the chair, had her meals, and just stared ahead of her, blankly.

Three days passed. Bessie took Aunt Blanche meals regularly but she never spoke. She didn't even say, "Thank-you." Then she started to fidget and kept glancing out of the window. She muttered to herself. "He'll be here soon, then I'll be out of this mess."

Bastien heard her mutterings and asked her if she wanted anything, or did she wish to talk. She still refused to speak.

Two days later, Basil did appear. Bobby Bunny had established a look out position from one of his garden sheds, and noticed the long grass moving near the back entrance of the Manor.

He watched and waited. Basil's cap, then his head, rose slowly from the grass. He looked all round him for some time, then cautiously moved towards the Manor.

Bobby wasn't sure what to do. If he ran to the Manor, Basil would see him and run off. If he stayed where he was, he could not warn Bastien.

What should he do?

At that very moment, the Post-mouse came cycling along the road and Basil, hearing the mouse whistling, ducked down for cover, back into the long grass.

Bobby seized his opportunity. While Basil was hiding, he could run the short distance to the Manor and went straight to Bastien.

"He's here," he gasped, just as a knock came at the front door.

Bastien answered the door. "Hullo, Mr Post-mouse. What have you got for me today?"

The Post-mouse handed over two letters, wished him a good-day, and rode off.

"Basil's in the long grass by the rear entrance," said Bobby.

"I hope he wasn't scared off by the Post-mouse," said Bastien. "Go back to your post and see if he is still there, will you?"

Bobby did as he was asked. He peered out through the door, but saw nothing unusual, then crawled across the garden, close to the hedges, on his hands and knees towards his shed, to hide himself.

He arrived at his post and looked out of the window. He could not see Basil anywhere. He was about to settle down in his usual look-out position, when the grass rustled at the rear of his shed.

He waited, all his senses straining in the direction of the grass. It went suddenly very quiet. Then the rustling began again. Bobby *had* to investigate. He crept out of the shed and turned the corner into the long grass and crawled right into ....

Thankfully it was only Beattie, his wife.

"What the devil are you doing here?" he whispered to her.

"What are *you* doing, crawling about on all fours? No wonder your trousers are always in such a mess," she retorted.

"I've brought your lunch, because you forgot to take it, and with all this messing about recently, early mornings and late nights, I just don't know where I am."

"Keep down," growled Bobby, "and keep you voice down."

"Don't talk to me like that!" interrupted Beattie, "I've just about had enough of all this nonsense."

"Basil's somewhere over there, near the gate," said Bobby, "and we are trying not to scare him off."

"It's about time you all grew up." snapped Beattie, "You think more of them Badgers, than you do of your own family."

"What time do you think you'll be home for your tea? That's supposing I take the trouble to make you any."

Bobby shrugged his shoulders. What was the point of arguing?

"Oh!" he said, "I expect I'll be home about 5 o'clock as usual."

Beattie left in a flurry, her long dress rustling in the long grass. "Just you mind you are too. I'm not wasting good food," was her parting remark.

Bobby went back into the shed and took up his position again and looked all around. There was no sign of Basil anywhere.

At a quarter to five, he remembered his promise to Beattie, and set off to see Bastien.

It took him less than a minute to reach the back door, which he entered. He saw Bastien by the inner door, went up to him and told him he was just off for his tea, but he would be back soon.

That was all he said, for, at that moment, a Badger jumped out from behind the door, and grabbed him.

Bobby felt a strong arm around his neck and the oily smell of a wax-jacket. It was Basil!

He suddenly dropped onto his right knee and pulled Basil's right forearm with both his paws.

He felt the weight of the Badger slide over his back and saw him land in the middle of the floor, rolling over and over in a ball and coming to a stop - *'thump!'* - up against a cupboard.

Bobby straightened up and tidied his ruffled clothing. His heart was beating quickly at his sudden reflex reaction.

A pair of green Wellington Boots appeared from out of the ball, found the floor, and the form of Basil stood up. It had all happened so quickly.

Basil made a lunge for Bobby, who side-stepped the attack and the Badger stumbled out through the door. He turned and came back to grab Bobby again. This time there was no escape.

He was so much stronger than Bobby, and was easily able to keep Bobby still, while Aunt Blanche tied his limbs with the same ties that Bobby had tied her up with.

Bobby shouted to Bastien for help, but Bastien had already been caught and tied up too, and could offer no assistance at all.

They were both herded into the lounge and tied together, back to back.

"I'm sorry about this," said Bastien, "but Basil must have come in through the back door, just after you left, found Aunt Blanche, and set her free."

"Aunt Blanche called out that she wanted to talk, so I went in to her. She was sitting exactly as we left her, with her arms behind her back. When I entered the room, she suddenly got up. It surprised me enough to be caught by Basil, who was waiting behind another chair."

"They knew you would come back, so they tied me up, stood me beside the doorway and waited. When you came through the door, well ...... you know the rest."

In the Bunny home, Beattie was fuming mad. She had been watching her clock. She turned to her eldest son, Bertie, and said, "Where's that good-for-nothing father of yours got to now. He promised he would be home by five o'clock and now it's a quarter past. I'll give him another five minutes, then I'm going up to the Manor."

Bertie replied. "Shall I run to the Manor and get him?"

Beattie, a little calmer now, having got her anger out of her system, said, "Not at the moment, we'll wait another five minutes, then you can go."

Those five minutes ticked slowly by and still no sign of Bobby.

"I'm going up to the Manor now," said Bertie, and called out to two of his brothers, "Do you want to come to the Manor?"

"O.K.," they replied, "We'll race you. The last one's a cissy."

"Try the sheds first," Beattie called after them as they all rushed out of the house and raced towards the Manor.

Bertie arrived first, but the other two were a very close second, and they started arguing who had lost. "It was you." "No it wasn't, it was you."

Bertie didn't stop to discuss who had won or lost, he was searching the sheds for his father.

He was nowhere to be seen. They knew where he had been, for they found his empty sandwich box in the shed with the gardening tools.

They searched round the Manor grounds, then the three Bunnies went up to the back door of the Manor, and knocked on it, lightly at first.

When no-one answered, they knocked much harder. Still no answer.

"What do we do now?" asked one of the Bunnies.

"I suppose we had better try the door to see if it is open," said the second, grasping hold of the handle.

"Remember what father has told us about entering someone else's house," said Bertie. "Knock again. Somebody must be in."

Once more they knocked and still no reply.

"All right, we've done what you said, now let's do it my way," said Butch. "I'm getting hungry and I'm not standing here all night, waiting for an answer."

He turned the door knob and the door opened.

What he didn't see was two black and white striped faces peering round the inner doorway, watching him as he walked into the kitchen.

Beattie turned the key in the lock.......

CHAPTER 5

BARADA RUNGARD!

Butch entered the kitchen cautiously. His senses were all alert, because he knew he was trespassing on someone else's property, and his father had always told the Bunnies not to go on property that didn't belong to them, without permission.

His eyes searched the kitchen, but no one was there.

The other two Bunnies watched him from the safety of the doorway.

They saw him go boldly through the inner door and heard him call out, "Is anybody here?"

Suddenly there was a scuffle, and Bunny fur flew everywhere. Butch cried out, "*Help! Help!* I've been caught. Barada Rungard!"

The other two Bunnies reacted immediately, but instead of running to help their brother, they bounded as fast as their little legs would carry them, back to their mother.

In the meantime, their captured brother had been put with his father and Bastien, in a side room.

"What are you doing here?" asked Bobby, quite surprised to see his son.

"Mummy sent us to find you, because you promised to be home for tea at five o'clock, and you never came. She's very upset and we offered to come and get you. I got caught, like you."

"How many of you came?" asked Bastien.

"Besides me, there's Bertie and Brent," said Butch.

"Where are they then, or are they caught as well?" asked Bobby.

"No. I managed to shout "Barada Rungard", and they ran off. I think they got away. Bobby smiled when he heard those words.

Bastien frowned. "What's Barada Rungard?" he asked.

"You will see," said Bobby smiling to himself, "You will soon see."

Bertie and Brent arrived home, explained what had happened and, immediately, the Bunnies were collecting together all their equipment.

"Off you go then," said Beattie, "Remember, you are a team, so work together as you've been taught. You've got to rescue your father and brother."

They marched up to the Manor, all twelve of them, and gathered at the back door.

They politely knocked on the door and waited for it to be answered.

Nobody came, but Basil had seen all the Bunnies approaching and saw them gathering at the door.

"What do we do know?" he asked his Aunt. "They have probably come for their father and brother. They're only small and look harmless enough."

"I suppose we could tell them that they have gone, and are not here. Perhaps they will go away. In any event, it will give us a chance to deal with Bastien and Bobby."

Blanche went to the door, but she never had time to open her mouth, for, as she opened the door, she was jumped on by four Bunnies, who knocked her over.

Before she had time to recover, she was overpowered by all the Bunnies and tied to a chair.

The Bunnies then dispersed throughout the Manor, looking for their father and brother.

One of the Bunnies called out "Koofounda" and when Bobby replied, they all gathered outside the room where Bastien, Bobby and Butch were imprisoned.

Beattie turned the key in the lock, opened the door, and released the three captives.

While Bobby and Beattie hugged each other, the other Bunnies had formed into two groups. Bertie led one of the groups and his next eldest brother, Biff, led the other.

They searched the manor from top to bottom, and found Basil Badger in one of the bedrooms holding his walking stick in both paws, like a barrier out in front of him.

He was ready to defend himself, as he had witnessed what had happened to his Aunt minutes earlier and *he* wasn't about to be overpowered by a handful of Bunnies, like she was.

"Now, Casta Torogo", said Bertie, quietly, so only the Bunnies could hear him.

His group moved to the left and Biff's group moved to the right.

Basil Badger raced between the two rows of Bunnies, prodding with both ends of his stick, first to the right, then to the left.

Bunnies began to fall in all directions as he ran through their ranks.

They were not hurt, only rolling out of his way at the last possible second, to confuse the Badger. It was all part of their training and strategy.

The first two Bunnies in each row, then rolled over and came to their feet behind Basil, the next two rolled under his feet, tripping him up, while the rest of the Bunnies jumped on him.

He managed to shrug them off, but the Bunnies regrouped in their two rows.

Basil attacked them again, this time waving his stick around his head, trying to hit the Bunnies. But he missed every time, as the Bunnies hopped and rolled about, scattering in all directions, to avoid the blows.

There were so many of them, and Basil was soon exhausted from the sheer physical effort needed to keep flailing his stick and his life, as an Estate Agent, had made him physically unfit.

Bobby noticed that Basil was weakening and called out, "Barada Getimo!"

As one, all the Bunnies jumped on Basil, knocking him over, and pinning him to the ground by their sheer weight of numbers.

Bobby tied Basil's hands behind his back and said. "Barada Orf!". Immediately the Bunnies left Basil and stood all round him.

"Well done, you Bunnies", said Bobby. "I am very proud of you. That was an excellent performance. I'm sure your grandfather would have been very proud of you as well."

Bastien had been watching all this happening in amazement. He'd never seen anything like their action before, certainly not by a family of Bunnies.

Badgers overpowered by Bunnies! That was quite an impressive achievement! Badgers were usually so tough and strong, and were not easily defeated by anyone. But the Bunnies had done it, not once, but twice!

"What were all those words you said?" wondered Bastien.

"Oh! It's only part of the Bunny survival system," said Bobby. "I'm glad we were able to help you regain the Manor."

"Yes, thank you all so very much," said Bastien. "I think you deserve a special treat." He gave each Bunny a silver coin, and they all thanked him.

"I think I can manage now," said Bastien. "You can all go home, and thank you again for your help."

Then Beattie arrived to find out what had gone on, and Bobby explained it all to her.

Satisfied, she called out. "Casta Torogo!" and all but two of the Bunnies, stood in two lines as they had done previously. She went to the front of the two lines and marched them triumphantly back home.

Bobby and his two eldest sons agreed to stay at the Manor that night, to guard Basil and Blanche Badger.

Bastien noticed Bobby was glancing at his watch. It was half-past six, and Bastien realized that Bobby had missed his tea, so he asked him and his sons to share his.

During tea, Bastien discussed the capture of his brother Basil and his Aunt Blanche, and Bobby wanted to know what he was going to do with them.

"We'll decide that in the morning, when I have a fresh mind to think with," said Bastien. "I've had enough excitement for one day with your army of Bunnies, and I need a little relaxation, as it's now all under control. I have been and collected one of the bottles of brandy from the chamber, and I think we should have a little celebration drink."

He opened the door and there stood Bobby Bunny.

CHAPTER 6

HEATED DISCUSSIONS

The next morning, Bastien asked Butch to go and ask Bessie Beaver if she would come to work at her normal time, and would Bobby and his other son like to start tidying the Manor grounds.

"Now then," said Bastien, addressing both his Aunt and his brother, who were still tied up. "We are all together and now is the time to settle our disagreements, once and for all."

"I want to untie you both, but I must have your solemn promises that you will not try to escape. This business over the Manor has to be resolved sooner or later, and this is as good a time as any. Do you both agree?"

The two Badgers looked at each other for a brief second and nodded quickly, then turned to Bastien and said, "Yes!"

Bastien stooped over his Aunt and started to untie her legs.

He sensed the tension in her legs and quite expected her to kick out at him. After all the trouble he had experienced with her since his father had died, he felt he couldn't trust her, even though she had given her word.

He stood up, leaving her still tied, and she asked why he had stopped. "Because you have tensed up and I don't trust you." He said.

"Oh! I've been in this position all night and need to stretch my legs," she sighed. "Don't worry, I promise not to escape." Bastien knew she meant it this time. The tone of her voice was that of defeat, but he only loosened the tie round her legs. Just in case!

"Bobby Bunny's outside with his family," lied Bastien, to make sure she didn't change her mind and try to escape.

She recalled how four of the little Bunnies had caught her off guard and tied her up the previous evening and that killed off any lingering thought of escape. She was quite placid and Bastien really felt that he could, at last, begin to trust her.

He didn't completely untie her arms, but loosened those knots as well, so that she could have a little more freedom.

He then turned to his brother Basil, and said. "Boots, I am disappointed in you. My own brother turning against me like you did. You really upset father, trying to sell the manor and with him still living in it. He couldn't leave the Manor to you. He knew you would get rid of it."

"But," said Basil, "father said he was tired of living here and hinted that he wanted to sell the Manor."

"As I'm an Estate Agent in the Big City, I could have sold the Manor at a very good price. I thought he meant it."

"You know father," said Bastien. "He often said things he didn't really mean. Do you really think he would have sold our home? He was very proud of our heritage, wasn't he? I didn't particularly want the responsibility of running the Manor, for I wasn't really interested in the country way of life. It's too slow with all those summer shows and events, although it *is* expected of us Badgers to lead the community."

"I wanted to do my own thing with the excitement of the pop-group at the time, but they were not very trustworthy, and now I've found that I quite like the way the animals live around here. Since the success of the party for Bessie Beaver, our housekeeper, I have grown really fond of the servants who work for us. They show a real, genuine dedication to their duties. Even you must have realized that, with Bobby and his family doing what they did to help me."

Basil recalled again how easily the Bunnies, and a handful of young Bunnies at that, had outwitted him yesterday, and had completely tired him out and easily overpowered him. No doubt his life style had a lot to do with that, but he had been caught!

Bastien continued. "I've come to realize they need the Manor as a place of work, and as a focal point for their village."

Blanche began to fidget on her chair.

"Do you think you could release Aunt Blanche?" asked Basil. "I think she's had quite enough of all this. She's not as young as she used to be, you know."

Bastien looked again at his Aunt. There was no more fire or fight left in her eyes and he untied her arms.

She immediately clipped him round the ears with her right paw, saying, "That's for tying me up and not showing any respect for your elders. If your father had seen how I've been treated, you would have been put across his knee and given a good spanking."

Bastien listened, and nodded in agreement.

"I'm sorry, Aunt Blanche, but the Weasels told me how you had encouraged all their attacks on the Manor. They showed me your letters, telling them about the secret entrance and everything else."

"The more I heard, the more I had to believe what they said, and it's very difficult to forgive you and forget what happened."

"Yes, you are right," said a saddened Aunt Blanche." I felt really guilty, but I was so annoyed at the Manor being left to you and not to your brother, 'Boots', that all family loyalty was forgotten, and I became determined to get the Manor for myself. I hoped to stay here with 'Boots' after he had inherited it."

"Well, as far as I was concerned," Bastien continued, "Basil *was* going to inherit the Manor. That's why I tried to make a career for myself."

"It came as quite a shock when I was told it was left to me, although father used to say it quite often."

"What could I do? I had to obey my father's last wishes."

"I had thought of asking you both if you wanted the place, but I knew Basil was living in the city and when he tried to sell it, I knew he wasn't really interested in living in the Manor."

"Then, when the Weasel attacks started, and I found out who was encouraging them, I decided to stay and fight it out. It was then that I realized that life is too short for all this continual squabbling."

"We would have gone on like this for years to come. None of us would have won, the family would have split up, and we would not have enjoyed our lives."

Basil was listening to his younger brother. The more he listened, the more his bottom jaw dropped in amazement at the wisdom that Bastien was speaking.

He shook his head in disbelief and said: "What stupid Badgers we have been. Whatever do the villagers think of us?"

"They never say anything about our problems," said Bastien, "at least, I've never *actually* heard them speaking about us, but they must be aware of what's been going on, although they probably don't know the whole truth about it."

"Well, what they don't know, they make up, so I wouldn't worry too much about what others think," said Basil caustically.

Bastien could feel some mutual trust developing between the three Badgers as the conversation was becoming easier and more friendly, and he was about to continue, when a '*Knock! Knock!*' came on the door.

He opened the door, and there stood Bobby Bunny.

"Could I have a word with you please?" he said. "Bessie Beaver has just arrived for work, and I've told her that you still have your Aunt and brother here at the Manor."

She wondered if the staff should come back to work as things appear to be back to normal.

Bastien put his left forearm across his stomach, then placed his right elbow in his left paw and stroked his chin with his other paw and began to think.

He said, slowly, "Ask Bessie if she could manage with just a few of the staff, just to tidy up the house and prepare meals."

"I suggest someone like Silvia Shrew and Perkins the Pine-Marten, and could Bessie make us some tea and bring us some biscuits now, please?"

Bobby passed the message to Bessie Beaver and she agreed to make the tea, then go and contact Silvia and Perkins.

Bastien returned to his brother and Aunt and continued to speak: "I've asked some of the staff to come back to the Manor, and I hope we can get back to normal very soon."

They ought to mind their own business!

CHAPTER 7

FINAL DECISIONS

Aunt Blanche had listened throughout the conversation and decided it was her turn to say something.

She cleared her throat with two sharp coughs and said, "I want to tell my side of the story."

"I've never been so badly treated as I have by young Bastien. He has shown me no respect, for he has tried to frighten me, by dressing up as his father, then he tied me up, not once mind you, but twice. I've been attacked by swarms of Bunnies, quite why I'm not sure. What right have they got to come barging into the Manor without being asked ....?"

Bastien raised a paw. "Aunt Blanche," he said, "you brought your troubles on yourself. You decided to kick me out of my own home, just because you wanted to live here with 'Boots', in-spite of what father said in his Will."

"That Will wasn't right," Aunt Blanche interrupted sharply. "It must have been changed when your father was ill following his fall last winter."

"That's not true," said Bastien, quite taken aback with that statement. "That's *certainly* not true. He changed his Will soon after Basil had tried to sell the Manor."

"I happened to remember what date was on the Will when it was read out. So I know you're not telling the truth there."

"That's a lot of rubbish!" retorted Aunt Blanche, raising her voice for all to hear, "Who told you that! I never heard the date read out at the reading of the Will."

Another *knock knock* came at the door, interrupting Aunt Blanche as she was about to continue.

Bastien opened the door. It was Silvia Shrew. She curtsied to Bastien and said, "Excuse me sir, but I have brought your tea and biscuits. Shall I put the tray on the table?"

Bastien stood to one side and beckoned Silvia to enter the room.

"Shall I pour the tea out now?" she asked.

"No thank you," snapped Aunt Blanche rather rudely, "I'll do that! Now be off with you." Silvia curtsied to Aunt Blanche and hurried out of the room.

"Steady on," said Bastien, "If we're going to argue, please not in front of the staff."

Aunt Blanche didn't like being corrected by her nephew and said," You're just like your father, no respect for your elders."

"I'm sorry," said Bastien, "respect is something that has to be earned in this life, and not taken for granted. We'll get nothing sorted out by shouting at each other."

Silvia Shrew had been listening outside the door, and could hear every word they were saying. She shouldn't have done that really, but anything she overheard, she could tell the staff. Bessie came up the stairs at the very moment that Silvia was leaning against the door with her ear pressed tightly to it.

"What are you going?" Bessie demanded to know. "Get to your work this minute. I'll talk to you later."

Silvia's face went red and she became flustered. She had been caught eavesdropping, trying to pick-up some scandal. She could never be trusted with a secret, as she told everyone about every little thing that happened at the Manor, and the arguments, that were going on between the Badgers, was exactly what she loved to spread about.

Bessie followed Silvia, and caught up with her at the bottom of the stairs.

"You had better go off home now," Bessie snapped angrily, "I'll finish up here."

"But it's early yet," said Silvia, "and I've not finished my work."

"Never mind your work," said Bessie firmly, "What goes on between the Badgers is their business and not for your ears. When you work for someone, you must respect their secrets and their privacy. I've told you before about this. Now off you go, and come back when you've had a long think about your future. I'll have to report your conduct to Bastien."

Bastien was unaware of all this and was still talking to his Aunt Blanche.

"Why did you get the Weasels involved in our problems?" he challenged his Aunt.

"Because they needed land for homes for their families and your father refused to allow them any, so it was easy to encourage the Weasels to attack the Manor, to get you out. But those Weasels are *so* stupid. They failed me every time. They couldn't even face up to your gardener, Bobby Bunny," she said, "I heard about him chasing them off with a garden fork."

"That Bunny family should never be under-estimated," said Bastien, chuckling to himself as he recalled that day. "If it wasn't for Bobby Bunny and his family, we wouldn't be talking here today."

"It's no laughing matter!, snapped Aunt Blanche, quite hurt that she had been let down by the Weasels, "Basil and I took a lot of trouble giving them information on how to get into the Manor through the secret tunnel. What with them and those Bunnies ...."

They remembered how Basil and Aunt Blanche had been over-powered by the Bunnies and Bastien remembered how, single-handedly, Bobby had repelled the Weasels with his garden fork, and again with the help of Bastien's spider costume, in the secret tunnel.

"No," said Bastien, holding up both hands, "I won't hear a bad word against the Bunnies, I have a lot to be thankful to them for."

"Poppycock!" said Aunt Blanche, "They ought to mind their own business."

"Well," said Bastien, "I respect their loyalty to me and the Manor and will not let you speak about them like that. It's a pity we Badgers don't have the same loyalty between ourselves, as the Bunnies have. None of this would ever have happened."

"Look," said Basil, "let's get this whole matter cleared up. We've all had our say now, and I think it's about time that we solved the problem of the ownership of the Manor."

Bastien quickly interrupted him. "There you go again. For once and for all, the Manor legally belongs to me. Our father Willed it that way and neither you, nor I, nor anyone else, can dispute that. We were all present when the Will was read. It's up to me what happens to the Manor. What I am prepared to do is to offer you both the opportunity to possibly buy it from me, or perhaps we could even share it somehow."

Basil looked slowly at Bastien. He was getting bored with all the bickering and slowly asked. "What do you want for it then?"

"Well, you're the Estate Agent. What's it worth?" replied Bastien.

Basil perked up at the sound of business. There was money to be made here. If he could buy the Manor cheaply, he knew that he could sell it, *and* get a good profit.

"Don't go thinking that you'll get it cheaply, said Bastien, anticipating Basil's thoughts by his reaction to the question. "I'm not that stupid. I've got a rough idea what it's worth."

"It's only worth what someone is willing to pay for it," snapped Basil, and Bastien knew he had read Basil's thoughts correctly.

"I don't want to see the Manor sold off," said Aunt Blanche. "It's been in our family for generations. I don't think our ancestors would take very kindly to that. Anyhow, I'd rather like to live here myself."

"How about if we all lived here?" suggested Bastien. "We are all one family. The Manor could be jointly owned by us all, or you could stay here as my guests for as long as you liked."

Basil agreed that that was a good idea, but he, personally, wished to continue with his work in the Big City, and he didn't really want to live in the Manor as he would soon lose touch with his business friends back in the Big City.

If he took a part-ownership, he would be liable for paying part of the bills as well.

Aunt Blanche had always wanted to live in the Manor, and now that Bastien was offering her the chance to, and for as long as she liked, she was ready to agree to Bastien's offer.

It was getting quite late by now, and Bobby Bunny came to the door to ask if he might go home, or did Bastien still want him to stay that night, in case of any more trouble.

"That's all right," said Bastien, smiling and taking Bobby's paw in his and shaking it firmly. "You get back to your family and apologize to Beattie for missing your tea, and thank them all, once again, for their help today. I will see you bright and early for work in the morning."

"We'll be safe here tonight, and I think everything is going to be O.K. from now on."

Printed in the United States
by Baker & Taylor Publisher Services